To my family,   with love –M.H.

First published in 2017 by Scholastic Children's Books
Euston House, 24 Eversholt Street, London NW1 1DB
a division of Scholastic Ltd
www.scholastic.co.uk
London ~ New York ~ Toronto ~ Sydney ~ Auckland
Mexico City ~ New Delhi ~ Hong Kong

Text and illustrations copyright © 2017 Matt Hunt

ISBN: 978 1407 15918 8
All rights reserved · Printed in Malaysia

10 9 8 7 6 5 4 3 2 1

The moral rights of Matt Hunt have been asserted.
Papers used by Scholastic Children's Books are made
from wood grown in sustainable forests.

Lion was
fed up.

Fed up of hustle
and bustle.

Bump and
shuffle.

Drip and **drizzle.**

Honk and **beep.**

Lion dreamed of clear skies and sunshine,
wind in his mane and sand in his paws.
Just him and his guitar.

This was his lucky day.
He spotted a beach house advert.

WEATHER

NEWS
CRASH!

FOR SALE
BEACH HOUSE

Lion packed his bag that very evening.
Top of the list was his favourite treat ...

... strawberry smoothies.
Lots of strawberry smoothies!

To get to his beach house,
Lion took **planes** ...

trains ...

and
automobiles ...

and cruised on a **cruise** ship.
Finally he could see, out of nowhere ...

... his **dream island.**
It was itsy-bitsy. It was comfy and cosy.
It was a beach paradise!

SOLD

No one can bother me here,
sighed Lion.

Each morning Lion woke to parrots
squawking and waves splashing.
He picked juicy coconuts for breakfast,
then strummed his guitar under the sun.

But life on the island wasn't all SO perfect.

Playing beach ball wasn't much fun with **one** player.

There was **no one** else to do the washing-up.

He didn't get even one birthday card. Lion was becoming ... **lonely.**

He stared out at the sea, trying not to cry.
"I need a **friend**," he whispered.
But he had no telephone and there was no postbox.
"I've got it!" he said,

"I'll send a message ...

...in a bottle!"

Looking for a friend...
Do you play the guitar?
Like strawberry smoothies?
Do you love sun, sea and sand?
Come join me on Desert Island.

Lonely **Lion**

"Well done, me!"
Lion smiled.

The bottle bobbed along, carried away by the waves.

Then Lion waited ...

... and he waited ...

But no one came.

"I know! More messages, more bottles!"
Lion roared. He counted his empty
strawberry smoothie bottles.

"1,
2,
3 ...
15 ...
60!"

Lion sat and watched until the very
last one disappeared into the sunset.

The next morning, as Lion was
still snoozy with sleep ...

... a penguin landed on his beach!

"Hello, my new friend! I got your message! Now, let's jazz things up and make some music!"

TOOOT

TOOOOOT

TOOT

TOOOOOOT!

TOOOOOOT!

TOOOOOOT!

"Is that a **saxophone?**" Lion shrieked. "That's **loud** and screechy! I wanted my new friend to bring a **guitar!**"

And he walked away and left the penguin all on his own.

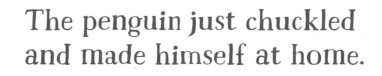

The penguin just chuckled and made himself at home.

And little by little, Lion began to love the sound of the new music.

One fine afternoon, Lion spotted something strange out in the sea. Were there more visitors to come?

"Hey, funky friends ...
It's showtime!"
bellowed a rhino.

"Well, HOWDY!" flapped a flamingo.
"Thanks for the message
in a bottle!"

"A piano and maracas," fussed Lion,
"I hate the sound of them."
So he **stomped** away,
hugging his guitar.

But the music drifted towards
Lion, and he couldn't help ...

... tapping his foot.

It was ... different ...

... and **noisy** ...

And
he
LIKED
it!

Lion raced to join in, and the new friends played
together until the stars began to twinkle and
the full moon bathed them all in its glow.

Soon, even MORE visitors arrived on Lion's island.

But now everything was different.
Lion couldn't wait for the new sounds, sights and fun.

"Come and join our band," Lion beamed.
"Let's boogie-woogie! Let's sizzle and shake!
Let's PLAY!"

The island was now the **loudest**, bounciest most swinging place *ever*.

There was **hustle** and **bustle**!

Bump and **shuffle**!

Clap and **cheer**!

Honk and **beep**!

And Lion ...?

Lion was **happy**, at last.